TALES FROM
BRAMBLY HEDGE

JILL BARKLEM

Collins

An Imprint of HarperCollinsPublishers

CONTENTS

This edition first published in Great Britain in 1997 by HarperCollins Publishers Ltd
This edition copyright © Jill Barklem 1997
Text and illustrations The Secret Staircase, The High Hills, Sea Story, Poppy's Babies
copyright © Jill Barklem 1983, 1986, 1990, 1994
Introduction copyright © Jane Fior 1997

ISBN 0-00-198279-6

3 5 7 9 10 8 6 4 2

Printed and bound in Italy.

THE STORY OF
BRAMBLY HEDGE

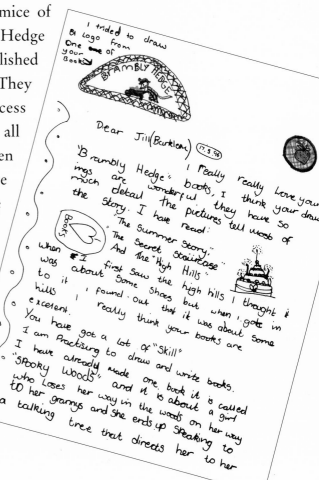

Jill Barklem's first four stories of the mice of Brambly Hedge were published in the autumn of 1980. They were an immediate success and appeared in editions all over the world. Children (and adults too), were intrigued by the miniature community portrayed with such loving attention to detail, and would write to Jill with questions and comments, and always asked when the next books would appear.

I trided to draw
a logo from
one of
your books

BRAMBLY HEDGE

Dear Jill (Barklem) 17.5.96

I really really love your "Brambly Hedge" books, I think your drawings are wonderful they have so much detail the pictures tell most of the story. I have read: "The Summer Story", "The Secret Staircase" And the "High Hills"

When I first saw the high hills I thought it was about some shoes but when I got in to it I found out that it was about some hills.

I really think your books are excelent.

You have got a lot of "Skill"

I am Practising to draw and write books. I have already made one book it is called "Spooky Woods", and it is about a girl who loses her way in the woods on her way to her grannys and she ends up speaking to a talking tree that directs her to her

THE STORY OF
BRAMBLY HEDGE

Although SPRING STORY, SUMMER STORY, AUTUMN STORY and WINTER STORY were published in a small format especially chosen to reflect the diminutive nature of the mice and their lives, they took Jill every available working hour to produce and by the end she was exhausted. The kind of visual concentration needed for such detailed illustrations is very tiring, and Jill, who had had problems with her eyes ever since she suffered a detached retina as a child, needed to take a rest from close work.

When she first embarked on the Brambly Hedge books, she and her husband David were living in a small house on the edge of Epping Forest. By the time the books were printed she was expecting a baby. Shortly after publication, Elizabeth was born. The new family now needed more space and so they moved to a slightly larger house in Epping, where they were closer to Jill's parents.

4

While Jill was concentrating on her baby, Collins
brought out a Brambly Hedge pattern book which
showed the nimble-fingered how to make little
replica mice from fur fabric. This was followed by a
poster book. The illustrations were even more
impressive when enlarged to show Jill's scrupulous
draughtsmanship – the flour mill that really worked,

the amazing
detail of the
numerous
little rooms
in Crabapple
Cottage.
Later there
was a book
of Brambly
Hedge tunes
for children
to play on
the recorder,
address
books and
diaries, and
before long

a full merchandise programme had been put into place. It was now possible to buy Brambly Hedge plates and cups and saucers, Brambly Hedge shampoo and soap. But in spite of the popularity of these items, what the public really wanted was more stories.

Jill had started work on the next four: THE SECRET STAIRCASE, THE HIGH HILLS, SEA STORY and POPPY'S BABIES. They were published individually in 1983, 1986, 1990 and 1994, and she was to discover that each one would present her with a special challenge.

Working on THE SECRET STAIRCASE meant that Jill experienced a fierce tug of loyalties. She wanted to spend as much time as possible with her new baby and yet she also wanted to get back to her inner world, the one into which she withdrew the minute she sat down to draw. Was it going to be possible to give both areas of her life the attention they required? She felt guilty towards her family when she worked; she felt a sense of obligation to her publisher when she didn't. And, of course,

6

there is a special fear that comes after success. Would she be able to maintain the standard and commitment that she achieved with the first four books?

There was no need for anxiety. When THE SECRET STAIRCASE was published in 1983, her waiting public were delighted with this new adventure that gave more prominence to two favourite characters, Wilfred and Primrose.

The next book, THE HIGH HILLS, again featured Wilfred, that intrepid explorer, and drew upon the Lake District for its background. Jill did much of her natural history research in the area and family holidays were combined with finding suitable streams, waterfalls and flora.

Another baby was on the way too. As Jill painted Wilfred and Mr Apple clinging to the ledge, it was hard to reach over to the drawing board.

7

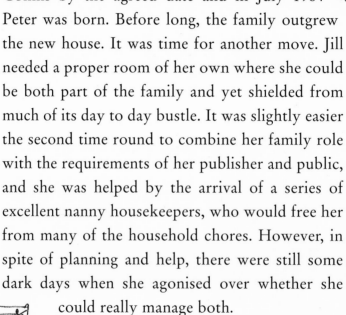

Again it was a race against time. Would she be able to complete the book before the new baby's arrival? She handed the artwork in to Collins by the agreed date and in July 1984 Peter was born. Before long, the family outgrew the new house. It was time for another move. Jill needed a proper room of her own where she could be both part of the family and yet shielded from much of its day to day bustle. It was slightly easier the second time round to combine her family role with the requirements of her publisher and public, and she was helped by the arrival of a series of excellent nanny housekeepers, who would free her from many of the household chores. However, in spite of planning and help, there were still some dark days when she agonised over whether she could really manage both.

In 1986 David, who had always liked sailing, suggested that they acquire a family boat, moor it near Ipswich in Suffolk and use it to spend time together away from the pressures of work and success. Jill was secretly appalled. She had visions of the children falling overboard, the boat being

blown out to sea, all hands lost...
It was hard to admit to such
fears and David's calm and
rational assurances were
not enough to dispel
Jill's alarm.

She decided that
the only way
forward was to
learn everything she
could about boats; she
diligently applied herself to the rules
of navigation and sailing, the demands of the
tides and the wind, shipping lanes and safety at sea.
As she began to inform herself, her fears abated and
so she was able to begin to enjoy their
leisurely excursions up and down
the Orwell. The children loved
these expeditions and, though
small, soon acquired natural good
sense as far as the water was
concerned.

9

To her surprise, Jill discovered a real interest in the sea which spilled over into Brambly Hedge. How *did* the mice get their salt? What route did they take and whose responsibility was it to make sure that the Store Stump always had an adequate supply? Little by little, the plot of SEA STORY began to unfold. Bemused staff at the National Maritime Museum may have exchanged glances when Jill asked if they knew how a mouse might make a compass of natural materials available in the British Isles, but once again her meticulous research and insistence on authenticity would underpin her work and enhance the illustrations.

POPPY'S BABIES, the book she had been looking forward to tackling ever since that first shy courtship on the river bank, was to prove the most demanding of all, for this time Jill would have to face a situation that would require all her faith and courage. As she worked on the illustrations, she

found that she was getting increasingly tired and her sight was presenting real problems. It was not just a question of eye strain this time – it was getting more and more difficult to focus, almost as if her vision was slipping away. As you will see, there is nothing to indicate this in the pictures themselves, but in fact by the time she reached the last illustrations she was only able to see half the page she was working on – the rest had simply disappeared.

THE STORY OF

BRAMBLY HEDGE

Appointments with various specialists were arranged and Jill went into hospital for neurological tests. This was a very worrying time, and the diagnosis more worrying still – Jill would need an operation to relieve pressure on the optic nerve. Although the surgeons were cautiously optimistic that her sight would then be restored, no one could be sure. As a naturally creative person, whose means of expression relies so entirely on the ability to record what she sees, this whole period was very frightening.

The operation was carried out and the news good. As soon as the pressure was removed, Jill's sight returned to normal but there was an enforced period of convalescence, and Jill had to postpone starting work on the first of a new series of books. As if in compensation, this was the moment when the story of Brambly Hedge took a new and exciting detour.

HIT Entertainment, a company that develops animated film versions of established children's

classics approached HarperCollins to see if there was any possibility of animating Brambly Hedge. The question had come up in the past but had been shelved because no one seemed able to achieve the degree of perfection that Jill would require. It was not that she was against the idea of film in principle, but she wanted to see the essence of the books truly captured and be convinced that everyone working on the project would respect her ideals and share her desire for authenticity.

Peter Orton, the managing director of HIT, and Kate Fawkes, his executive producer, presented their ideas to Jill. They wanted to make four separate films of the first four books, and as they spoke, it became clear that they had grasped the particular qualities of Jill's work and had spent time finding the most appropriate film makers and techniques. From their point of view, they recognised that their potential audience already knew the books inside out. They had to find a way to animate Brambly Hedge that would be true to the original work and not disappoint readers, whether they be children or adults.

One of the first decisions they had to make concerned the kind of animation. Should it be model or cel? Cel animation, the method most usually associated with children's features, requires that everything is drawn by animators, either by hand or with the aid of computer techniques. Model animation has a completely different quality but can be very effective because it is three dimensional.

They decided that model animation was the most suitable medium and proposed Cosgrove Hall, a studio in Manchester responsible for the highly successful THE WIND IN THE WILLOWS. The chosen team headed by producer Jackie Cockle had the necessary skills to create a rich and believable world and would enjoy the challenge of Brambly Hedge.

Jill agreed. She had always felt that if a film were to be made, she would prefer to see the mice presented as models. She was anxious about cel animation and not convinced of the wisdom of using other artists to recreate her work. Then when she met Bridget Appleby, who would be artistic director of the film, she was doubly convinced.

Here was a kindred spirit. Bridget too had a special feeling about the natural world and already knew

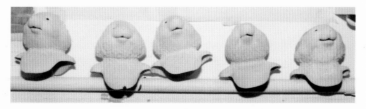

Jill's books. She suggested that model animation, used in conjunction with Jill's own drawings, was the solution. Instead of using the illustrations simply as reference for the animation, they could become part of the film. Bridget explained how she would use a multi-layered technique called decoupage to give them a three dimensional feel so that when seen in context with the model mice, there would be no sudden impression of a flat background.

Describing her technique later, Bridget said, "I decided to make the sets look a bit like a giant pop-up book. I'm glad I didn't know at the start the number of sets that would be needed – it turned out to be fifty-seven!"

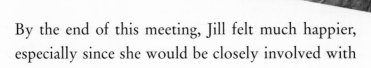

By the end of this meeting, Jill felt much happier, especially since she would be closely involved with

the films at all stages. Jackie and Bridget went back to Manchester to organise two minutes of footage so that Jill could see for herself just how Bridget's proposal would work. The same piece of film would then be shown at the forthcoming trade fair in Cannes to interest British and foreign television companies in the series.

It usually takes at least two years to produce one of Jill's books, sometimes more. In the film world, things have to move quickly. As soon as Jill had approved the trial video tape, all the various aspects involved in the creation of the films had to be put in place. First of all came the 'treatments'. Kate Fawkes worked with Jill's original editor, Jane Fior, to see how each of the stories could be extended to fit a half hour slot. It was important to retain the essence of each text, but also essential to find ways to build on the basic plot so that there could be more action and more scope for the individual characters. Once done, these treatments were handed over to Jocelyn Stevenson, an experienced script writer for children, to develop. The casting of the voices was already underway, so

that as soon as the scripts were ready they could be recorded. Robert Lindsay, Neil Morrissey, Charlotte Coleman, Jim Broadbent, June Whitfield, Michael Williams, Rosemary Leach, Anton Rodgers, Alun Lewis and Noreen Kershaw were approached and all agreed to take part.

The texts of the original books are quite short and the personalities of the different mice are built up by nuance and gesture. Was it difficult for Jocelyn to bring them to life? "The first thing I did was to immerse myself in Jill's work, to the point where I could close my eyes and imagine myself walking through the hedge. Then all I had to do was watch and listen. I began to hear the characters in my head, and once that happened, I got to know them, and the things they would or wouldn't do – which would eventually make up a plot – became obvious."

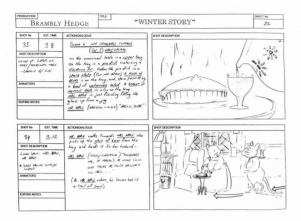

Jill approved the direction the scripts were taking and as soon as they were ready and recorded, they were handed back to Cosgrove Hall.

The recordings then had to be carefully 'bar-sheeted' which means that the voices are broken down frame by frame (with twenty-five frames per second of film), so that the animators could work with these in conjunction with the assembled voice track which was on audio cassette. This done, it was time for Jackie and the team to prepare the storyboards. In these the action, timing and camera angles for every shot are worked out in advance.

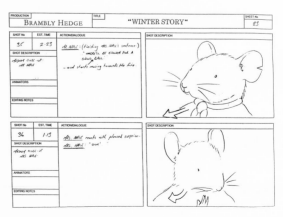

19

Meanwhile, the model makers were already at work on the mice. One of the main challenges was to ensure that each mouse looked different – and looked like him or herself. If you look at the films carefully, you will see how successful they have been. Each mouse has a slightly different head and body shape and manages to closely reflect Jill's original conception. Jill was able to describe the mice in further depth so that, for example, the fact that Mr Apple walks with a limp, the result of an earlier injury, was a vital piece of information in establishing his character.

When it came to clothing, although probably it would have been possible to use coloured fabric, in fact both colour and designs were hand-painted onto white material with watercolours in order to reproduce that soft, well washed look that they have in the original illustrations. The mice themselves, each about 9 inches high, were first sculpted in clay

p 59

39.
Simple. fang
vandneck. Orann in
at chest.

20

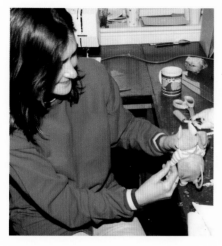

and then moulds were taken and rubber latex skins cast. Fur fabric was considered as a treatment but rejected. There was a danger that the models would look too much like soft toys and that they could get damaged during production.

Music is also an important part of an animated film and this too had to be commissioned early on. Jill wanted an authentic English country sound and Ernie Wood, a composer who works a lot for television and who, as it happens, lives in the middle of a forest, was asked to compose the theme music for Brambly Hedge, as well as a number of jigs and waltzes and Wilfred's birthday whistle tune.

THE STORY OF

BRAMBLY HEDGE

Theresa Plummer-Andrews, the head of Children's Acquisitions and Creative Development, had bought the series for the BBC and decided to show the four films on a seasonal basis, starting with WINTER STORY. When the team heard that the programme would go out at 4.15 in the afternoon of Christmas Day, they were elated. This was the best possible slot and a real mark of appreciation for the quality of the film. In the event, over seven million adults and children watched Wilfred and Primrose extricate Basil from his snowy predicament, and praise began to flow in. By this time, deals had been struck in America, Germany, France, Scandinavia, Italy, Poland, Mexico, and Australia, and many more were in negotiation around the world. Brambly Hedge, already internationally established in book form, was now repeating its success on film, justifying HIT's original decision to embark on one of the most expensive model animation series ever mounted.

All this seems a long way from Jill's tiny workroom overlooking the garden. Without a telephone,

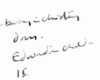

22

it represents a sanctuary from the world. All the surfaces are crammed with sketches, notebooks, her natural history research, photographs, dried leaves and flowers, paints, inks, pens and brushes. Now that she has completed eight books, and the challenge of a film adaptation has been successfully accomplished, what is to follow?

"I want to explore the way of life in Brambly Hedge in more detail. The supportive and co-operative philosophy of the mice seems very enviable to me. I'd like to discover more about the mechanics and theory that underpins their society. It's as if I've been able to open a little door into an ideal world and am allowed to peep through. My task is to faithfully record what I see. This is my next challenge."

JANE FIOR

THE SECRET STAIRCASE

It was a frosty morning. The air was crisp and cold
and everything sparkled in the winter sunshine.
The little mice hurrying along the path turned up
their collars and blew on their paws in an effort to
keep warm.

"Merry Midwinter," panted Dusty Dogwood,

scurrying past Mr Apple and the Toadflax children with
a huge covered basket. Mr Apple and the children were
busy too, dragging great sprays of holly and trails of ivy
and mistletoe towards the Old Oak Palace. When they
arrived at the gates, they heaped all the branches on the
ground and Wilfred tugged on the bell.

Lord Woodmouse and Primrose, his daughter, opened the door.

"Here we are," said Mr Apple, mopping his face, "do you want it all inside?"

"Yes, please," said Lord Woodmouse. "We'll start by decorating the stairs." Eagerly, the children pulled the branches over the polished palace floors and skidded their way into the Great Hall.

"Are you two ready for tonight?" asked Lord Woodmouse.

Primrose and Wilfred exchanged glances. That evening, after dark, all the mice would gather round a blazing fire for the traditional midwinter celebrations. A grand entertainment was planned and Primrose and Wilfred had chosen to give a recitation.

"Almost," said Primrose, "but we've still got to practise and we need proper costumes."

"You'd better see your mother about those," replied her father. "You can practise wherever you like."

Leaving Clover, Catkin and Teasel to go back to the wood with Mr Apple, Primrose and Wilfred took themselves off to a corner of the hall and began to go through their lines.

"*When the days are the shortest, the nights are the coldest…*" began Primrose, drawing an imaginary cloak around her.

"*The frost is the sharpest, the year is the oldest…*" continued Wilfred.

"Look out, you two," interrupted Basil, bustling past with some bottles.

"This is hopeless," sighed Primrose. "We can't rehearse here. Let's go and ask Mama what to do."

Lady Woodmouse was busy making caraway biscuits in the kitchen. She leaned on her rolling pin to listen to Primrose's tale of woe.

"Why don't you see if there's something up in the attics for you to wear," she said. "You could practise up there too." She packed a little basket with bread and cheese and a jug of blackberry juice and shooed the children gently out of the kitchen.

There were a great many attic rooms at the top of Old Oak Palace. Lady Woodmouse used them to tidy away things that might come in useful. Babies' blankets and rolls of lace, boxes of buttons, stacks of books, broken toys, patchwork quilts, pudding cloths and old saucepans were all crammed together, higgledy-piggledy, on the shelves.

Primrose and Wilfred went from room to room looking for a suitable spot for their rehearsal. They ended up in a crowded storeroom at the end of a passage, but it was difficult to concentrate on practising, there were so many things to look at.

Standing on tiptoe, Primrose reached inside the drawer of an old wooden dresser. In it, she found some bundles of letters tied up in pink ribbon but she couldn't read the writing and as it's rude to read other people's letters, she put them back. As she did so, she caught sight of a small key which had slipped down at the side of the drawer.

"Look at this, Wilfred," she cried excitedly.

"Let's see. Oh, it's only an old key," said Wilfred. "Is it time for lunch?"

Primrose said nothing, but she slipped the key into her pinafore pocket before setting out their picnic on the floor.

"Do you think this would make a cloak?" said Wilfred, his mouth full of bread and cheese. He had seized the end of a long green curtain and was winding himself up in it. As he turned towards Primrose, he caught sight of a small door hidden behind its folds.

"Where does this go to, Primrose?" he asked.

"I don't know," replied Primrose, scrambling over some boxes. "Does it open?"

Wilfred pushed. The door was locked. He peeped through the keyhole and saw another flight of stairs on the other side of the door.

 "It's no good," he said, disappointedly, "we can't get in."

 "If there's a keyhole, there must be a key," said Primrose, "and I think I have it here!" She reached inside her pinafore pocket and handed the little key to Wilfred. He tried it in the lock. It fitted perfectly and the door swung open.

They found themselves in a dark panelled hall
at the foot of a long winding staircase. The stair
carpet must once have been beautiful, but now
it was tattered and covered with dust.

"No one can have been up here for years and
years," whispered Primrose. "Shall we see what's
at the top?"

Wilfred nodded, so up the stairs they went,
round and round. Primrose kept close behind
Wilfred, she couldn't help feeling a little nervous.
Suddenly the stairs came to an abrupt end. They
were standing in yet another hall, and there ahead
was yet another door, but this time it was huge
and richly carved. They went up to it and Wilfred
gave it a push. As the door opened, the children
stared about them in amazement.

They were standing in the most magnificent room. There were columns and carvings, and dark tapestries and paintings on the walls. In front of them two golden chairs stood on a little platform. Everything in the room was covered in dust and the air smelled musty and strange.

"Where are we?" asked Wilfred.

"I don't know," whispered Primrose. "I've never been here before."

They tiptoed across the floor, leaving footprints as they went.

"Maybe your ancestors lived here in the olden days, Primrose," said Wilfred, gazing at an imposing portrait.

"Let's clean it all up and have it as our house," said Primrose. "We could keep it secret and come up here to play."

As she spoke, she opened a cupboard and found it full of hats.

"Wilfred! Look at these. They're just right for tonight!"

A door at the end of the room led into a nursery. There was a canopied cot near the window, and all sorts of dust-covered toys were on the shelves.

Wilfred peered inside an ancient trunk and pulled out a little suit with a high jacket and tight braided trousers. It was almost the right size for him. Neatly folded beneath it were dresses and cloaks, waistcoats and shawls, some trimmed with gold and others studded with shining stones. The children held them up, one after another, and each chose an outfit for the evening and tried it on.

"Perfect! And now we must practise."

"Let's finish exploring first," said Wilfred.

They seemed to be in a whole suite of rooms. There was a dining room, a butler's pantry, a small kitchen and several other bedrooms. The bathroom was particularly grand with a tiled floor and high windows. Wilfred rubbed a mirror clean and made faces at himself whilst Primrose leaned over the side of the bath to try the taps. No water came out.

"When the days are the shortest, the nights are the coldest…" she recited. Her voice sounded loud and echoey. Wilfred joined in, and they went through their lines again and again until they were word-perfect.

Outside the red sun was sinking low in the frosty air, and the bathroom was filled with shadows.

"It's getting late," said Primrose. "If we don't hurry, we'll miss the log."

They picked up their clothes and scampered over the dusty floors to the door.

Down the stairs they ran, round and round, down and down, till they found themselves back in the storeroom. They locked the door with the

little key and replaced it in the drawer. Then they
crept along the corridors to Primrose's room,
taking care to keep out of sight.

Primrose opened her window. They could just hear the carolling of the mice as the midwinter log was pulled along the hedge. There was no time to change, so they threw on their cloaks to hide their costumes and ran to join the crowd at the palace gates.

Mr Apple and Dusty Dogwood headed the procession, lanterns held high.

"Roast the chestnuts, heat the wine,
Pass the cups along the line,
Gather round, the log burns bright,
It's warm as toast inside tonight,"

sang the mice as the log came into view.

Teasel, Clover and Catkin were perched on the huge branch and as it was dragged up to the palace gates, Primrose and Wilfred scrambled up behind.

The mice pulled the log carefully over the threshold and Basil threw some bramble wine onto the bark. "Merry Midwinter!" he called.

At last the log was here. The midwinter celebrations could begin.

A fire had been laid ready in the hearth of the Great Hall and the log was rolled onto it. Everyone was handed a cup of steaming punch. Old Mrs Eyebright was to light the fire, and she held up a burning taper.

"To Summer!" she announced and Mr Apple stooped to help her thrust the taper into the fire.

"To Summer!" echoed the mice.

The bright flames licked the mossy bark and soon the log was ablaze. The mice helped

themselves to supper which was spread on a table
near the fire and Basil refilled their cups.

"Why don't you take off your cloak, dear?" said
Lady Woodmouse. "It's very hot here by the fire."

"Not just yet, Mama," said Primrose. "I'm still
a bit chilly."

When they had eaten all
they could, they drew
their chairs up round
the hearth and the
entertainment
began. Mr Apple
made huge shadows
on the wall by standing in front of the fire. He
made the shape of a weasel with a mean little eye,
and a snake's head, a fox, and with
the aid of a curtain, a bat. The
little mice squealed and laughed.
Next, Basil played a jig on
his fiddle and Dusty did some
conjuring tricks. Then they tried
to pass a crabapple
right round
the circle,
holding it under their chins,
and after that Lord Woodmouse
told stirring tales of olden times.
Primrose and Wilfred nudged each other.

Everyone did a turn until at last Lord Woodmouse said, "And now Primrose, what have you got for us?"

The children jumped up and took their places in front of the fire. Drawing their cloaks closely round them, they began:

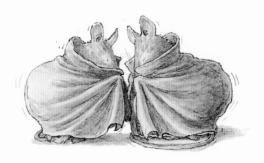

MIDWINTER

When the days are the shortest, the nights are the coldest,
The frost is the sharpest, the year is the oldest,
The sun is the weakest, the wind is the hardest,
The snow is the deepest, the skies are the darkest,
Then polish your whiskers and tidy your nest,
And dress in your richest and finest and best...

For winter has brought you the worst it can bring,
And now it will give you
The promise of SPRING!

Primrose and Wilfred threw off their cloaks and
donned their hats with a flourish. The audience

gasped to see the beautiful clothes which sparkled
in the firelight, and then clapped and cheered
louder than ever. The applause went on for so long
that Lord Woodmouse had to ask them to do it all
over again.

At last, Primrose and Wilfred went back to their seats.

"That was wonderful!" whispered Lady Woodmouse, hugging her. "*Wherever* did you find those beautiful clothes?"

Primrose glanced quickly at Wilfred. "In the attic," she mumbled, hoping that her mother would not ask any more awkward questions. Luckily, at that moment, Basil started to tell one last story and everyone settled down to listen.

Primrose and Wilfred gazed at the fire and thought of all the lovely games they would play in their house at the top of the secret staircase. Soon their heads began to nod and in no time at all, they were both fast asleep.

THE HIGH HILLS

It was the very end of autumn. The weather was damp and chilly and Wilfred was spending the day inside with the weavers. *Clickety, clack* went the loom, *whirr, whirr* went the spinning wheel. Lily and Flax were in a hurry.

"We must finish in time," said Flax. "We promised Mr Apple."

"What are you making?" asked Wilfred.

"Blankets," replied Lily.

"Who are they for?" said Wilfred.

"They are for the voles in the High Hills," replied Flax. "They have just discovered that the moths have eaten all their quilts and they've no time to make new ones before the cold weather comes. They're too busy gathering stores for winter. We're helping out."

"Can I help too?" asked Wilfred.

"That's kind of you, Wilfred, but not just now," said Lily. "Why don't you find yourself a book to read while I finish spinning this wool?"

Wilfred went over to the bookcase. On a shelf, tucked between volumes on dyestuffs and weaves, he found a thick book called *Daring Explorers of Old Hedge Days*. He settled himself comfortably and began to turn the pages.

"Sir Hogweed Horehound," he read, "determined to conquer the highest peak of the High Hills, for there, he knew, he would discover gold. Alone he set forth, taking in his trusty pack all he needed to survive the rigorous journey..."

Wilfred sat entranced. The whirr of the spinning wheel became the swish of eagles' wings, the clatter of the loom, the sound of falling rock, and the drops of rain on the window, jewels from the depths of some forgotten cave. Was there really gold in the hills beyond Brambly Hedge, he wondered.

Suddenly a door slammed. It was his mother
come to fetch him home for tea.

"I hope he hasn't been too much trouble," said
Mrs Toadflax.

"He has been so quiet, we'd almost forgotten
he was here," said Lily. "You can send him down
again tomorrow if you like."

Lily and Flax were already hard at work when Wilfred arrived the next morning. He settled down by the window again to read about Sir Hogweed Horehound and his intrepid search for gold.

The morning flew past and by the time Mr Apple arrived to collect Wilfred, Flax and Lily had almost finished the cloth.

"I'm sorry we couldn't match the yellow," said Flax. "We've used the last of Grandpa Blackthorn's lichen and no other dye will do."

"Never mind," said Mr Apple. "It's the blankets they need. We'll take them up to the hills tomorrow."

"The hills," repeated Wilfred. "Are you really going up to the High Hills?"

"Yes," replied Mr Apple. "Why?"

"Can I come?" Wilfred asked desperately. "Please say I can."

"Oh, I don't think so," said Mr Apple. "It's too far. We shall have to stay overnight."

"I'll be very good," urged Wilfred.

Mr Apple relented. "We'll see if your mother agrees," he said. "Come on, young mouse. It's time to go home."

To Wilfred's surprise, his mother did agree.

"It will do him good to be in the open air," she said. Wilfred rushed upstairs to pack. He knew just what he would need. Sir Hogweed Horehound had listed all the essential gear in his book: rope, a whistle, food, firesticks, cooking pots, a groundsheet and blankets, a spoon, a water bottle and a first-aid kit.

"And I had better have a special bag for the gold," said Wilfred to himself as he gathered everything together.

He went to bed straight after supper. It was a long way to the High Hills and to get to the Voles' Hole by dusk, they would have to make an early start.

Next morning, soon after dawn, Flax, Lily and Mr Apple called for Wilfred. They were carrying

packs on their backs, full of cloth and blankets,
and there was honey and cheese and a pudding
for the voles from Mrs Apple. Wilfred hurried
down the stairs.

"Whatever have you got there?" asked Flax.

"It's my essential gear," explained Wilfred.

"You won't be needing a cooking pot. I've
got some sandwiches," said Mr Apple.

"But I must take everything," said Wilfred.
His lip began to quiver. "How can I find gold
without my equipment?"

"You'll have to carry it then," said Mr Apple.
"We can't manage any more."

The first part of the journey was easy. The four mice went up the hedge, past Crabapple Cottage, the Store Stump and Old Oak Palace. Then they rounded the weavers' cottages and arrived at the bank of the stream. Carefully they picked their way over the stepping stones and clambered up into the buttercup meadow.

Wilfred strode through the grass, occasionally lifting his paw to gaze at the distant peaks. Beyond the bluebell woods he could see the path begin to climb.

Mr Apple looked back. "How's my young explorer?" he said. "Ready for lunch?"

"Oh, please," said Wilfred, easing off his pack with relief.

The mice ate their picnic and enjoyed the late autumn sunshine but soon it was time to go on. All through the afternoon they walked. The path became steeper and steeper, and when they looked behind them, they could see the fields and woods and hedges spread out far below.

By tea-time, it was getting dark and cold, and the hills around were shrouded in mist. At last they saw a tiny light shining from a rock beneath an old hawthorn tree.

"Here we are," said Mr Apple. "Knock on the door, Wilfred, will you?"

An elderly vole opened it a crack. When she saw Mr Apple, she cried, "Pip! Fancy you climbing all this way, and with your bad leg too."

"We couldn't leave you without blankets, now could we," said Mr Apple.

The mice crowded into the cottage and were soon sitting round the fire, drinking hot bilberry soup and resting their weary paws.

For Wilfred, the conversation came and went in drifts and soon he was fast asleep. Someone lifted him gently onto a little bracken bed in the corner and the next thing he knew was the delicious smell of breakfast, sizzling on the range.

Wilfred ate heartily, oatcakes with rowanberry jelly, and listened to the voles describing their hard life in the hills. He was disappointed when Mr Apple announced that it was time to leave.

"Can't we explore a bit first?" he begged.

"Flax and I have to get back to work," said Lily, "but why don't you two follow on later?"

"Well," relented Mr Apple, "there are some fine junipers beyond the crag..."

"And Mrs Apple *loves* junipers," said Wilfred quickly, "let's get her some."

So the mice said goodbye to the voles and Mr Apple and Wilfred set off up the path.

Wilfred ran on ahead and was soon round the crag. When Mr Apple caught up with him, Wilfred was half way up a steep face of rock.

"Wilfred!" cried Mr Apple. "Come down."

"Just a minute," shouted Wilfred. "I've found something."

 Mr Apple watched as Wilfred pulled himself up onto the narrow ledge and started scraping at the rock and stuffing something in his pocket.

"Look!" cried Wilfred. "Gold!"

"Don't be silly, Wilfred," shouted Mr Apple. "That's not gold. Come down at once."

Wilfred looked over the side. His voice faltered. "I can't," he said. "I'm scared."

Mr Apple was exasperated. "Wait there," he shouted. Slowly he climbed the steep rocks, carefully placing his paws in the clefts of the stones. The ledge was very narrow. "We'll edge along this way. Perhaps the two paths will meet,"

he said. "We certainly can't go down the way we came up."

As they walked cautiously along the ledge, an ominous mist began to rise from the valley.

"If only we had some rope," said Mr Apple. "We ought to rope ourselves together."

Wilfred put his paw in his pack and produced the rope! Mr Apple tied it carefully round Wilfred's

middle and then round his own. And it was just as well for a few minutes later they were engulfed in a thick white fog.

"Turn to the rock face, Wilfred, we'll ease our way along, one step at a time."

They went on for a long time, then they took a rest. As they sat on the wet rock, the mist parted for a few seconds, just long enough to show a dee strange valley below.

Mr Apple was worried. He had no idea where they were. It looked as though they would have to spend the night on the mountain. It would be very cold and dark, and all he had in his pocket were two sandwiches the voles had given him for the journey down. His leg was feeling stiff and sore too. What was to be done?
He explained the situation
to Wilfred.

"It's all my fault,"
said Wilfred, "I didn't
mean us to get lost. I
just wanted to find
gold like Sir Hogweed."

"Never mind," said Mr Apple. "We must look for somewhere to spend the night."

A short way along the path, the ledge became a little wider. Under an overhang of rock a small cave ran back into the mountainside.

"Look," cried Wilfred, slinging his pack inside. "Base camp!"

Mr Apple sat gingerly on the damp moss at the mouth of the cave. Everything felt damp, his clothes, his whiskers, his handkerchief.

"I wish I'd brought my pipe, we could have made a fire," he sighed. "Never mind, we'll huddle close and try to keep warm."

But Wilfred was busily searching in his pack again. Out came the firesticks and the tinderbox. "I'll see if there's some dry wood at the back of the cave," he said enthusiastically.

"Wilfred," cried Mr Apple in admiration, "you're a real explorer."

Soon they had a cheerful blaze on the ledge outside the cave. Wilfred produced two blankets and the mice wrapped themselves up snugly while their clothes dried in front of the fire. The little kettle was filled from the water bottle and proudly Wilfred set out a feast of bread and cheese and honeycakes.

"You know," said Mr Apple, as he settled back against the rock. "I haven't enjoyed a meal so much for years."

To while away the time, Mr Apple began to tell Wilfred stories of his adventurous youth, and as they talked, the mists gradually cleared and a starry sky spread out above them. All was quiet but for the murmur of a stream which ran through the valley below like a silver ribbon in the moonlight. Warmed by the fire, they became drowsy and soon fell asleep.

The next morning they were woken by the sun shining into the cave.

"It's a beautiful day," called Wilfred, peering over the ledge, "and I can see a path down the mountain."

Mr Apple sat up and stretched his leg. It still hurt. "We'll have to go down slowly, I'm afraid," he said.

"Is it your leg?" said Wilfred. "I can help." And he brought out a jar of comfrey ointment from his first-aid kit.

They packed up and set off down the path. Mr Apple did the best he could but his leg was very painful. He managed to get as far as the stream but then he stopped and sat on a boulder with a sigh. "I can't go any further," he said. "What are we to do?"

The two mice sat in silence and watched the water swirl past the bank.

"Don't worry," said Wilfred, trying to be cheerful. "We'll think of something."

Suddenly he jumped up. "I've got it," he cried excitedly. "We'll *sail* down the stream!" He ran to the bank and with his ice-axe, he hooked out some large sticks that had caught behind a rock in the water. Using his rope to lash them together, he made a raft. "Come on," said Wilfred, "we'll shoot the rapids!"

"Are you sure this is a good idea?" said
Mr Apple. "Wherever will we end up?"

"Don't worry," said Wilfred. "It's all going
to be all right."

Carefully they climbed onto the raft, Mr Apple
let go of the bank and they were off!

They were swept to the middle of the stream
as it raced down the mountainside, twisting and
turning, sweeping and splashing, careering over
rocks and cutting through deep banks.

"My hat," shouted Wilfred. "I've lost my hat."

"Never mind that," cried Mr Apple, "just hold
on tight. There's a boulder ahead."

Wilfred gripped the sides of the raft, and
somehow they managed to keep the raft, and
themselves, afloat.

Down by the stream, Dusty was ferrying a search
party of mice over to the buttercup meadows when
he suddenly caught sight of a small red hat floating
along on the current.

"Look there," he shouted. All the mice peered
over the side of the boat.

"It's Wilfred's hat," cried out Mrs Toadflax.
"Whatever can have happened to him?"

"Can he swim?" asked Mrs Apple anxiously.

Meanwhile Wilfred and Mr Apple were beginning
to enjoy their trip on the river. The ground had
levelled out and the pace of the stream had become
gentler. They looked about them with interest.

"Wilfred," called Mr Apple, "can you see what I
can see? I'm sure that's our willow ahead."

Wilfred stared at the bank. "It is!" he yelled.

"And there's the Old Oak Palace and the hornbeam. This is *our* stream!"

As they rounded the bend, they saw the Brambly Hedge mice climbing out of Dusty's boat. At the very same moment, Mrs Apple looked up and cried, "Look! Look! There they are!"

The mice turned in amazement; the raft was almost abreast of them.

"Quick," shouted Dusty, "catch hold of this rope and I'll haul you to shore."

As the two mice clambered out of the raft and up onto the bank, they all hugged each other.

"Wilfred, you're safe," cried Mrs Toadflax.

"My dear, what has happened to your leg?" said Mrs Apple.

Lord Woodmouse took charge. "Come on, everybody," he said. "Let's get these travellers home and dry, and then we can hear the full story."

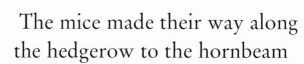

The mice made their way along the hedgerow to the hornbeam tree. Soon everybody was sitting round the fire, eating cake and drinking acorn coffee.

"Now tell us exactly what happened," urged Flax.

"Well, it was my fault," explained Wilfred again. "I was looking for gold and I got stuck. Mr Apple had to rescue me and then we got lost. And Mr Apple's leg hurt so much, we had to come back on the raft."

"Did you find any gold?" interrupted Primrose.

"No, only this silly old dust," said Wilfred, pulling the bag out of his pocket. Flax and Lily gasped.

"Wilfred! That's not dust. That's Grandpa Blackthorn's lichen. It's very rare. You *are* clever! Wherever did you find it?"

Primrose ran to fetch some paper and Wilfred proudly drew a map so that they could find the place again.

"And when we go, you shall come with us, Wilfred," promised Lily.

Mr Apple was tired and soon he and Mrs Apple went home to Crabapple Cottage. One by one, the visitors drifted away. It was time for the explorer to go to bed.

Wilfred followed his mother up the stairs.

"What adventures!" she said, washing his face and paws and helping him take off his muddy dungarees.

Wilfred climbed into bed. As his mother tucked him in, he thought of his night beneath the stars and snuggling down under his warm blankets, he was soon fast asleep.

SEA STORY

Primrose woke early that summer morning. She dressed quickly and tiptoed down to the kitchen. Her mother was already up, packing a rain cloak and hat into a small bag.

"Off you go," she said. "Take this apple to eat on the way. We'll see you later to say goodbye."

Outside the sun was already warm, and a light breeze stirred the leaves and branches of Brambly Hedge.

"Perfect," said Primrose, "just right for an adventure."

She ran across the field, through the long grass and down to the stream. There she found Dusty, Poppy and Wilfred hard at work, loading provisions on to Dusty's boat.

"Here you are at last," said Dusty. "I was beginning to think we'd have to leave you behind."

Wilfred helped Primrose carry her bag down the steep wooden steps to the cabin below.

"Look at this!" he said, pointing to an ancient yellow map spread out on the chart table.

"Does it show where we're going?" she asked.

"Yes," said Dusty, "it's the old Salters' map. Here's our hedge, and we've got to sail all the way down this river," he pointed to a wiggly blue line, "to the sea!"

On the bank a small crowd of mice had gathered to see them off.

"Will they be all right?" asked Mrs Apple anxiously. "Dusty's never sailed so far before."

"Look, my dear," said Mr Apple, "if the sea mice can manage to get the salt all the way up to us, I'm sure Dusty can sail downstream to fetch it."

"I can't think why we've run out," said Mrs Apple. "It's never happened before. Perhaps I shouldn't have salted all those walnuts."

"Stop worrying," said Mr Apple. "Look, they're about to leave."

"All aboard?" called Dusty. He hoisted the sail, cast off and turned the *Periwinkle* into the current. The voyage was about to begin.

The fresh breeze took them quickly downstream.
Primrose and Wilfred stood by the rail and waved
until everyone was out of sight, and then ran to
explore the boat.

They each chose a bunk, Primrose the top one,
Wilfred the one below, and stowed away their toys
and clothes. Then they hurried back up to help
Dusty with the sails.

Poppy prepared a picnic lunch which they ate
on deck, watching the trees and riverbanks as they
passed by.

"The wind's getting up," said Dusty, as he
cleared away, "make sure that everything's secure."
At that moment the boat began to heel to one side,
and an apple bounced to the floor.

"Can I steer?" Wilfred asked.

"Not in this wind, old chap."

"We're going rather fast," said Poppy.

"Yes, we'll be there in no time," said Dusty
cheerfully, hauling in on the ropes.

All afternoon the boat sped along, past rushes, trees and fields.

"Look out for a sheltered spot where we can moor up for the night," said Dusty. "I don't like the look of that sky."

"Will this do?" asked Poppy as they rounded a bend in the stream. Dusty turned the *Periwinkle* in towards the bank, and Poppy threw a rope around a twisted root to make it fast.

They were all glad to go below deck to get warm. Poppy lit the lamps, and heated some soup on the stove.

After supper, they sat round the table telling stories and singing songs until it was time for bed. The children, tired after all the fresh air, snuggled happily into their bunks. Outside, the water lapped the sides of the boat, and rocked them gently to sleep.

Next morning, Primrose woke to the sound of
the wind rushing through the willows on the bank.
Poppy was already up, making toast. Dusty and
Wilfred were at the chart table, studying the map.

"You'll need to dress warmly today," said Poppy.

Soon the sails were up and they were on their
way again. Wilfred helped Dusty on deck, and
Primrose looked out for landmarks for Poppy
to find on the map.

The day went quickly as the boat skimmed
along down the river. By tea time the children
had decided to become explorers.

"Look out! Sea Weasels!"
shouted Wilfred.

He jumped into the cockpit,
tripped over a rope, and knocked the
tiller from Dusty's paw. Dusty grabbed for it, but
too late – the boat swung round and headed for
the bank. There was a dreadful scraping noise and
the boat stopped dead. They had run aground.

"We'll *never* get to the sea now," wailed
Primrose. Wilfred hung his head; he felt close
to tears.

"Sorry, Dusty," he muttered.

"We won't get off this evening," sighed Dusty,
trying to lever the boat away with an oar. "We'd
better go below and have supper."

The sound of heavy rain greeted the mice next morning. When Dusty looked through the porthole he saw that the water level had risen during the night and floated them clear.

"Hooray," he shouted, and dashed up on deck to take the tiller. "Fetch the map; I think we're nearly there."

Primrose pointed ahead. "Look, that must be Seagull Rock. I can see some boats."

As they drew closer, they saw some water shrews fishing on the bank.

Dusty cupped his paws. "Are we on course for Sandy Bay?" he called.

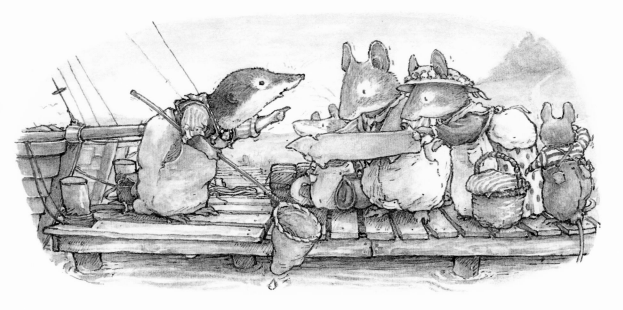

"Best anchor here and take the path up to the cliffs," said the water shrew.

Dusty moored up neatly between the other boats and the four mice stepped ashore. Slowly they made their way up the steep path through the pine trees.

At last they stepped up to the very brow of the hill, and there, spread out before them, glittering in the afternoon sun, was...

...the sea.

"It's so big!" gasped Primrose.

"And so blue!" added Wilfred.

One after another, clutching at tufts of marram grass for support, they slithered down the path.

"Which way now?" asked Primrose.

Dusty looked at the map. "To the right," he said, "past the sea campions."

Poppy was the first one to catch sight of a group of mice sitting by a door in the sandy cliffs.

"Excuse me," she called, "we're looking for Purslane Saltapple."

"Well, that's me!" replied one of the mice.

Dusty, delighted, ran to shake his paw. "We're from Brambly Hedge," he explained. "We've run out of salt."

"Then it's a fair wind that blew you here," said Purslane. "Let me introduce my wife Thrift, and our children Pebble, Shell and baby Shrimp."

"You must be exhausted," said Thrift. "Come inside, do, and make yourselves comfortable. I expect you'd like to wash your paws."

She led them down a passage to the bathroom. "This is the water for washing," she said, pointing to a pitcher on the floor. "If you'd like a drink, come along to the kitchen."

Poppy and Dusty's bedroom looked straight onto the sea. Primrose and Wilfred were to sleep in the nursery.

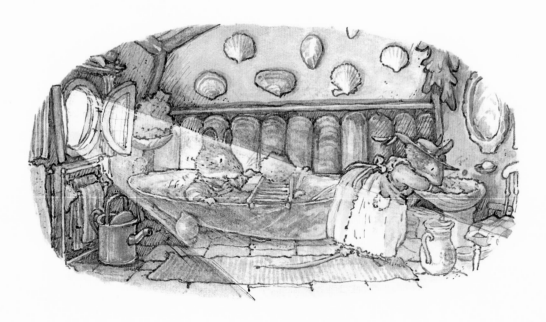

Poppy left them to unpack and went to find
Thrift. She was busy in the kitchen, rinsing some
brown fronds in a colander.

"Have you ever tasted seaweed?" she asked.

"No," Poppy replied, "but I'm sure it will
be very interesting to try it."

Soon they were sitting round the table, and trying their first taste of seaside food.

"What's this?" asked Wilfred warily, prodding the pile of vegetables on his plate.

"Marsh samphire, of course," said Pebble.

"Do I have to eat it?" whispered Wilfred.

Poppy coughed and quickly asked, "How long have the Saltapples been here, Purslane?"

"Our family has lived in this dune for generations. A long, long time ago our ancestors left the Green Fields and settled here. We've never been back, and I've often wondered what it's like."

At this, they began to tell each other about their very different lives in the hedgerow and by the sea.

"I've brought you a few things from Brambly Hedge," said Poppy, fetching her basket. Mrs Apple's honeycakes and strawberry jelly tasted strangely sweet to the Sea Mice, and the candied violets had to be put out of the baby's reach.

"Bedtime, children," said Thrift. "If it's fine, we'll go to the beach tomorrow."

As soon as they were up, the children wanted
to go straight to the sea.

"You'd better wear sunhats," said Thrift. "It's
going to be hot. We'll take a picnic and spend the
day there."

While Pebble and Wilfred built a sand palace,
Shell and Primrose
hunted for treasure
in the rock pools,

and Shrimp raced along the shore, getting in everyone's way.

The grown-ups spread out the picnic cloth, and reminisced about friends and relations as they watched the children play.

Suddenly, Poppy noticed that the waves were starting to creep up the beach, and she called the children back to the dune.

"It's the tide," explained Purslane. "It goes out and comes in twice every day. Soon the beach will be covered with water. It's time to go home."

On the third day, Wilfred woke to see dark
clouds rolling in over the sea. Purslane hurried past
the nursery door, pulling on his waterproofs.

"I've got to get the salt pans covered before the
storm breaks," he cried. "Come and help!"

They ran through a tunnel to the back of the
dune and out into the rising wind. Purslane paused
to hoist up a red flag, and they scrambled down
through the rough grass to the salt marsh. Wilfred
could see two huge dishes in the ground. One of
them was covered and the other open to the sky.

Purslane ran to release a lever and struggled to push the cover from one dish to the other.

"What's in here?" shouted Wilfred.

"We put seawater in one pan," said Purslane, "the sun dries up the water and leaves the salt for us to collect. The other one is to catch rainwater for us to drink."

Just as they finished lashing down the cover, the rain swept in from the sea. By the time they got home, huge waves were crashing on to the beach, and spray spattered against the windows.

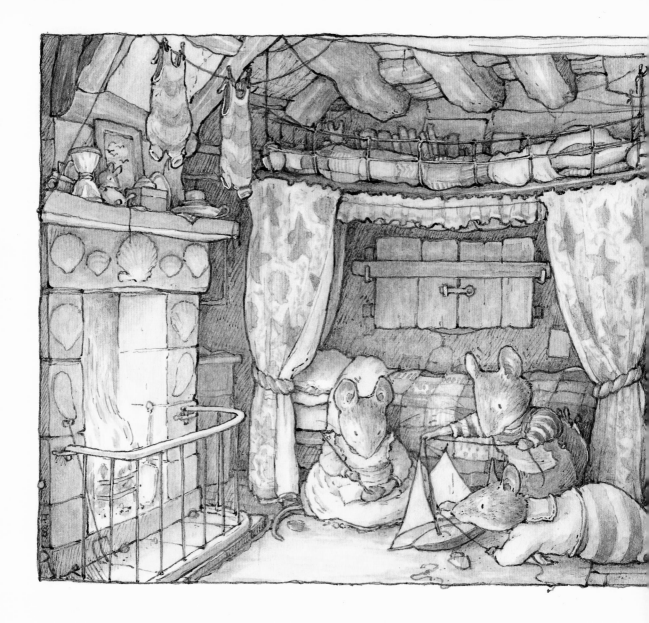

It was dark inside the house. Thrift lit the fire
in the nursery and trimmed the lamp.

"Sometimes we have to stay in for days and
days," said Shell.

"Especially in the winter," added Pebble.

The children played dominoes and five stones
and made pictures with seaweed.
Pebble helped Wilfred make a little boat with
real sails and rigging, and Primrose painted a
beautiful stone mouse as a present for her mother.

The storm blew itself out in the night. As soon as he got up, Purslane felt the seaweed by the front door and held up his paw to check the wind.

"It's set fair for your journey home," he said.

"Then I think we should be off as soon as we can," said Dusty.

"We must fetch the salt up from the store," said Purslane. "Will three barrels be enough?"

While their parents were busy, the children went off to play hide-and-seek in the maze of tunnels under the dune. They hid in storerooms full of pungent seaweed, behind jars of pickles and roots, and heaps of glistening shells.

"Let's go down to the storm bunker," said Pebble when he had found them all. He led them to some cold dark rooms deep in the heart of the dune.

"We come down here when it gets really rough," said Shell. "It's safer."

"Where are you?" called Thrift faintly. "It's time to leave."

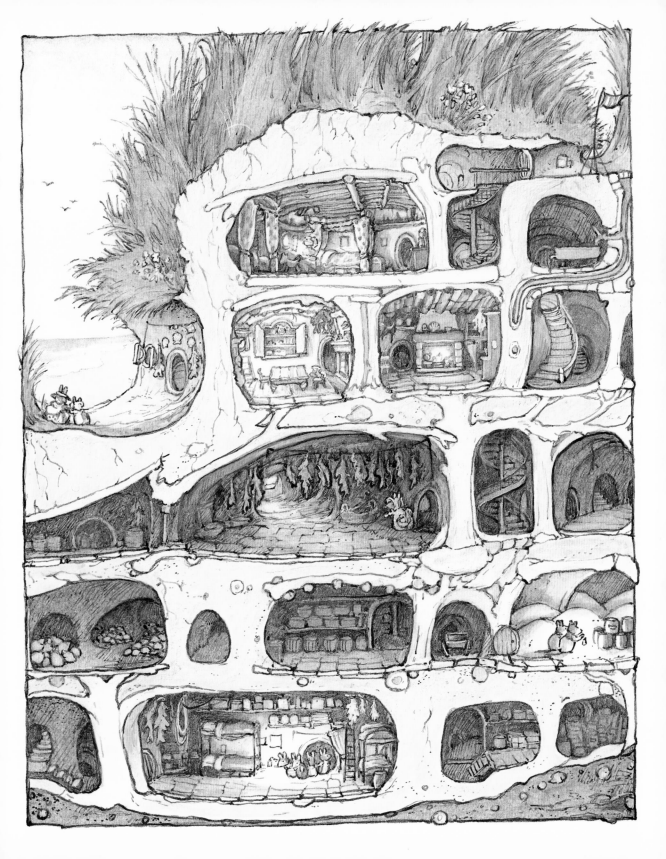

Reluctantly, Primrose and Wilfred went to the nursery to collect their things. Wilfred tied his boat to his haversack and put his collection of stones in his pocket. Primrose stood and gazed out of the window. "I don't want to go home," she said.

"We've a present for you," said Pebble quickly. "This is a special shell. Every time you hold it to your ear, you'll hear the sound of the sea and that will remind you to come and see us again."

Dusty and Purslane loaded the barrels of salt on to a handcart, and laden down with luggage and gifts, the little party set off along the dune.

They scrambled down the cliff path to the *Periwinkle* and with some difficulty loaded everything on board.

"Keep that salt dry, mind," said Purslane.

"Try and visit us one day," said Poppy. "We'd like to show you Brambly Hedge."

"All aboard!" called Dusty.

"And no stowaways," added Poppy, lifting Shrimp out of a basket.

They hugged their new friends goodbye, and thanked them for all their help. Poppy loosened the mooring ropes and Dusty hoisted the sail. He steered the boat into the stream once more and Primrose and Wilfred waved until Shell and Pebble were out of sight.

"I'm a salter on the salty sea
A' sailing on the foam,
But the salter's life is sweetest
When the sail is set for home,"

sang Wilfred as a fresh breeze caught the sails and swept them round a bend in the river.

POPPY'S BABIES

It was the beginning of summer. Outside, the trees were in leaf and sunshine sparkled on the stream. The millwheel turned in the cool shadows of the riverbank and inside the mill Dusty Dogwood was busy grinding the corn for the mice of Brambly Hedge.

Poppy was upstairs trying to persuade her new babies to go to sleep but every time they closed their eyes, the clatter of the mill shook the floorboards and woke them up again.

She opened the door to the stairs and a cloud of flour dust blew into her face.

"Dusty, please finish soon. It's time for the babies' nap."

"I'll do my best," he called back.

The babies were still awake when two visitors peeped round the door.

"Do you know that there are ninety-two stairs up to your kitchen?" gasped Primrose.

"However do you manage with the babies?" asked Lady Woodmouse, giving Poppy a kiss.

"It's very difficult," Poppy replied. She looked as though she was about to cry.

"How sweet they are," said Lady Woodmouse. "This one looks just like Dusty."

"That's Rose. Here is Buttercup, and the little one is Pipkin."

"I can't wait for their Naming Day," said Primrose. "When is it?"

"Just two days away!" said Lady Woodmouse.

At last the millwheels stopped turning and the babies slept. The visitors tiptoed out and Poppy sat down to rest. She was exhausted.

Dusty bagged up the flour and went over to the Store Stump. He found Mr Apple sitting at his workshop door, putting the finishing touches to a wooden mouse on wheels.

Wilfred, who was meant to be helping, was finding it much more amusing to play in the wood shavings.

"Hello, Dusty," said Mr Apple. "How are those babies of yours?"

"Noisy," laughed Dusty, "but great fun. Poppy is not so happy though. The mill is a very inconvenient place to live. It's noisy, dusty and damp and has far too many stairs."

"Come and live at our house," offered Wilfred.
"My mother loves babies."

"Thank you, Wilfred, but I fancy your mother
has enough on her hands with the four of you."

"I wonder what we can do to help Poppy," said
Mr Apple sympathetically.

Dusty returned later in the day to collect some wood for a repair to the mill.

"Come with me," said Mr Apple. Dusty and Wilfred followed him to a little cottage in a hawthorn tree next to the Store Stump.

"I've never noticed this house before," said Dusty.

"It's been empty for years. I use it to keep my timber dry," said Mr Apple.

While Dusty chose a suitable plank, Wilfred peered at an old cooking range.

"Does this still work?" he asked.

"I expect so," said Mr Apple. "It used to be very cosy when my aunt lived here." Suddenly he raised a paw. "Dusty, Wilfred has given me an idea. Suppose we clean the cottage and paint it. Would it suit you and Poppy?"

Dusty thought for a moment and then he said excitedly, "You know, I think it might!"

"Poppy would love this," Dusty said, looking at a small sunny room. "It's just the right size for a nursery."

"Let's get everything ready for Naming Day," said Mr Apple. "Do you think we can keep it a secret?" He looked pointedly at Wilfred.

"I won't say anything," said Wilfred. "Promise."

Mr Apple and Wilfred
went off to Crabapple
Cottage to tell Mrs Apple
about the plan and
Dusty hurried home to help give
the babies their bath.

"Look," cried Poppy.
"Buttercup's learnt
to crawl."

Dusty lifted her up and gave her a hug.

"I do wish we lived somewhere else," said
Poppy. "I have to watch them every minute
of the day."

Mrs Apple had alerted all the mice along the hedge and early next morning they began to arrive at Mayblossom Cottage with buckets and brooms. The windows were opened wide and the floors swept, sanded and scrubbed. Mrs Apple wiped down the dresser shelves and cleaned out the cupboards and Mrs Toadflax polished the bath. Dusty lit a pile of twigs in each grate to check that the chimneys weren't blocked.

"Now for the whitewash," said Mr Apple. "Do you want to mix it, Wilfred?"

"As soon as the walls are dry, we can start to fetch the furniture from the mill," said Dusty. "But how can we do that without Poppy seeing?"

"Ah, Mrs Apple's thought of a plan," said Mr Apple.

The next day Lady Woodmouse and Poppy sat
under the hedge, sewing. Bees buzzed in and out
of the flowers in the early morning sunshine and
the scent of hawthorn blossom filled the air.

"There, that quilt's finished," said Lady
Woodmouse, putting the last stitch into a yellow
flower.

"I've still got Pipkin's gown to make," sighed
Poppy. "However am I going to finish it in time?"

"We've had a good idea," said Lady
Woodmouse. "Why don't you all come and stay
at the Palace with us tonight. We can work on
the gowns together and Primrose can help you
to dress the babies for Naming Day tomorrow
morning."

"That would help Dusty too," said Poppy.
"He seems to be very busy at the moment."

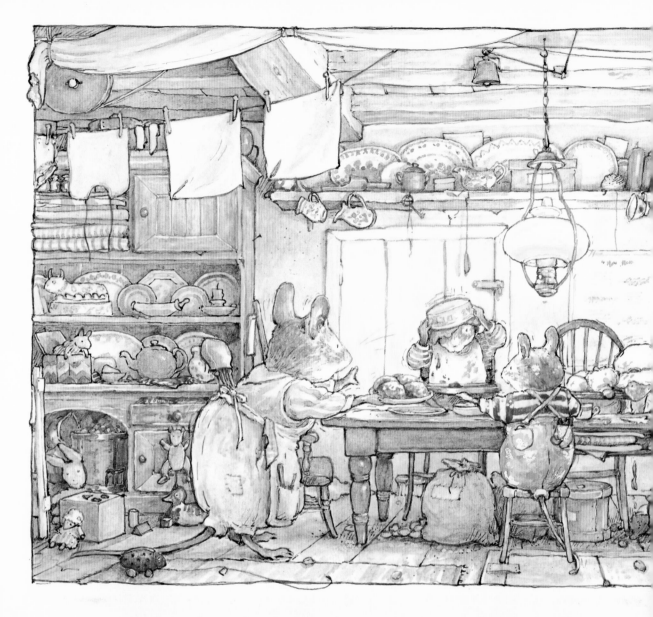

By late that afternoon, the cottage was almost ready.
Wilfred put a last coat of whitewash on the nursery
walls and Dusty measured up for the furniture.

"There, everything fits," he said with satisfaction.
"Let's go back to the mill for tea."

"Goodness, whatever have you two been doing?"
asked Poppy, staring at Wilfred's fur.

"Painting," said Wilfred proudly. "I mean..."

"Something for the babies," said Dusty quickly.

"You are a kind mouse, Wilfred," said Poppy.

Up and down Brambly Hedge, the mice were
all busy. In the Palace kitchen, Mrs Crustybread
was making a special cake and her daughter
Cicely made rosepetal butter and creamy junket.

Over at Mayblossom Cottage, Mrs Toadflax
had laid the table and was now hanging curtains,
while up in the nursery, Lady Woodmouse
unpacked the three little quilts.

"We're ready to fetch Poppy now," she said.

"Right," said Dusty. "As soon as you're at
the Palace, we'll start to move in the furniture."

Down at the mill, Poppy was busy packing.

"There seems to be so much to take," she said, folding up three little nightgowns. "Perhaps I should stay here after all."

"No, no," said Lady Woodmouse hastily. "Primrose will be so disappointed if you don't come."

Eventually, they managed to get the nappies, bottles, toys, prams and babies down the stairs (all ninety-two of them!) and were ready to set off to the Palace.

The babies loved the journey. Rose gurgled
when she saw the stream, Pipkin threw his rattle
in the water and when they reached the field,
Buttercup tried to get out of the pram.

At the door of Old Oak Palace, Dusty kissed
his family goodnight.

"Don't wait up for me," he said, "I've one
or two things to sort out before tomorrow."

The babies were bathed and put into their nightgowns. They were so excited by their new surroundings that they didn't want to settle but at last they all fell asleep in the quiet of the hedgerow evening.

Lady Woodmouse lit the lamp, then she and Poppy sat and stitched the last of the lace on to the babies' gowns.

"How peaceful it is here," said Poppy.

As she spoke, a curious squeaking, bumping noise came through the open window.

"Whatever is that?" Poppy asked, startled.

Lady Woodmouse got up quickly and drew the curtains.

"Just Lord Woodmouse tidying up," she said. "We'd better get to bed. We'll need to be up before first light tomorrow."

Very early next morning, all the mice gathered
beneath the hawthorns for the Naming Ceremony.
As dawn broke, Poppy handed Old Vole the first
baby. Primrose held up a cup of dew, freshly
gathered from the flowers, for Old Vole to sprinkle
on the baby's head.

"The buds on the branches blossom and flower,
The blackbirds sing in the leafy bower,
And over the hill comes the rising sun,
To shine on the fields, and on you, little one."

"We name you Rose," said Old Vole, gently.

Just as Old Vole named the last baby Pipkin,
the mice heard the patter of raindrops on the leaves.

"Oh dear, we'll all get wet," cried Poppy.

"No, no. Come this way," said Lady Woodmouse.
"Bring the babies."

Poppy and Dusty ran towards the Store Stump
and Dusty stood aside to let Poppy take shelter
in the open door of a cottage.

Poppy found herself in the kitchen. Bright china
that looked rather familiar was arranged on the
dresser shelves and garlands of flowers hung
from newly washed beams.

"What a dear little house," said Poppy.

"Let's look round," said Dusty.

Leaving Primrose in charge of the babies, Poppy
and Dusty climbed the stairs.

"It's so cosy," she said as they reached the
landing. "I wonder who lives here?"

Dusty led her to a small room that was warm
and bright. Fresh curtains hung at the windows
and beneath them stood three little cots, each with
its own embroidered quilt. One was pink, one was
yellow and one was blue.

"But Dusty..." she cried.

"Yes," said Dusty, "with love from all your friends in Brambly Hedge. Welcome home!"

Poppy threw her paws round Dusty.

"This is the nicest surprise I've ever had," she said, then she ran downstairs to thank each mouse in turn.

"It's time to cut the cake!" shouted Wilfred.

Everyone was given a large slice and Basil served a summer punch with flowers floating on top. There were cowslip and violet salads, rosepetal sandwiches, primrose pottage and meadowsweet tea.

The babies crawled around underfoot and Poppy was glad of Mr Apple's gates on the stairs. Then they were given some cake and got very sticky. Soon Rose began to cry, followed by Buttercup, and Pipkin rolled under the table.

"Poor babies, you're tired," said Poppy. "I'm going to put you into your cots."

The baby mice snuggled under their new
quilts and by the time Poppy bent to kiss them,
they were fast asleep. She tiptoed back downstairs
to join the guests in the kitchen.

Mr Apple proposed a toast.

"To the babies," he whispered, "and their
new home."

"To Rose, Buttercup and Pipkin," added
Mrs Apple. "Bless their little whiskers."